I0537494

CARAMBOLAGE

DOUG STEWART

AN EVEN MONEY BOOK
LOS ANGELES

Even Money Press
Los Angeles
evenmoney.press
First Edition. August 2019
ISBN 978-1-7334939-0-1
Copyright © 2019 by Doug Stewart
All rights reserved.

I sail the *Mare Serenitatis*

.

PREFACE

there are no right decisions,
only panicked reactions

This marks the third time I've wandered over here looking for inspiration. This time around I found a few poems and epigrams, several dreams, and a handful of conceptual pieces. The French have a useful word for this sort of thing, this *carambolage*, this mash-up of things unrelated in any significant way other than by chance [most commonly used to refer to a multi-car pile-up], or, as in this case, careening imagination.

Los Angeles
August 2019

CONTENTS

THE ORDER IN WHICH THEY CAME

Angular Shapes [1]

Swirling insect nimbus—
suddenly, darting angular shapes
in the silver-blue light.

Dark Glade Path [2]

wheeling about the solstice—

a few summer weeks
new dusk
new dawn
a few scant hours

soft shadows
edgeless
ill-defined
walking the dark glade path

attuned
this antique mood
archaisms and folkish practice
only now do we notice

Secret Hours [3]

Secret pre-dawn hours;
late evening's lingering mystery.

Erase the night?
Swallow the day?

It's when the mystery pales,
the secret hours beckon.

Intimate, I knew the night,
but once in flight, sought the day.

Emptied world not yet filled.
Strike; find the way.

Respite [4]

Summer's finally winding down.
Cooler evenings, soft breezes, violet shade;
the indistinct outlines of overhanging trees,
my wandering street lost in the hazy distance.

Repose. Peaceful exhaustion.
Just enough time to savor a few more sweet
days of respite before autumn, when the pace
quickens and the world steps forward in stark relief.

L.A. Folklore [5]

Mid-October's red flag warning;
already the jacaranda litter my driveway.

It's mythic L.A. folklore [Chandler, Didion],
this enervating, baleful wind.

Low humidity with clearing skies and rising
temperatures; these bright days and warm nights.

Though soon, perhaps even tonight, I'll smell
the smoke; an arroyo, a hillside, engulfed in
wind-driven flame.

Wanting to see, it's up to the ridge top [Knobhill,
Round Valley, Sumac, Deervale] where soft
brown foothills, deeply creased mountains, and
an endless carpet of human habitation are sharply
etched in late afternoon sun.

Shimmered And Swayed [6]

The wind blew all night, gusting, rising and falling,
buffeting my house [moonlit bobbing shadows crossed
my walls, the siding creaked; when I got up to check
the back porch it was a tree limb rubbing against the
screen].

I stood on the back step upright among scattered silent
moments and intermittent lulls. There, up on Flagstaff,
the brightly lit annual Christmas star. Nothing but long
strings of bulbs strung among tall poles, but in the middle
of my empty night it shimmered and swayed with a graceful
motion [side to side; up and down].

Enveloped, reassured by the onrushing wind's rising
warmth [the dehydrating snow now drifts of Styrofoam],
in my solitude [in a world emptied of human concerns]
I was able to capture a few rare moments of serenity.

A Sail in the Wind [7]

We stood high on an earthen dam for a country lake [dry by
then, abandoned to future developers of suburban tract-
wastes]; a Front Range chinook night of bright full moon,
racing streamers of thin wind-driven clouds, and my long
winter coat luffing in the wind like a sail. It's a vivid memory,
how I leaned into the wind to maintain my balance, that vast
expanse of open landscape, so drunk, so intoxicated with the
raging wind and the exhilaration of being there in that
moment, so … well, do bear with me, I *am* hunting for them,
but apparently I don't have the necessary words to capture that
x. No surprise. Can't articulate everything.

Hollowed Out Night [8]

rushing wind
hollowed out night

hissing whistling
shaking shook car

pinging grains of sand
windshield ricochets

in their wake
a million sparkling pits

Skittering Leaves [9]

skittering leaves
blustering wind
bobbing shadows
flickering jack-o'-lantern on the front porch

Modest Headwater [10]

Up the valley there's a spring in a shallow draw, and though it's
rarely more than a seep it's proven reliably constant. It's where
milling cattle have punched big holes in the soggy ground, the
grasses lush but puddled. Frozen in winter, one might easily
stumble walking such ground, but with the thaw the puddles
fill, the grasses green, and one finds surer footing. Almost
hidden, this modest headwater, the source for what comes
downstream.

Crispin Corner [11]

By now it's late afternoon,
the humid air has softened
until it's almost comfortable.
A high haze blunts the sun
leaving oncoming evening's
shadows faint and indistinct.
I run the windows down to
savor the earthy scent of plants
thriving in rich soil at the end
of a hot summer's day.

I follow the narrow road as it twists
and turns, running first along one
old farmstead and then another
before halting at a crossroads.

I check my map: Crispin Corner.
Left? Right? It's right. Down a
gentle hill and across an antique
concrete bridge spanning a small
stream where the air feels thicker,
cooler. When I look, off to my
right I see fireflies flashing in the dusk.

Sleep Never Found Us [12]

Late evening;
we're sitting under the cottonwoods
[by the irrigation ditch; we often did].

A car, tires softly crunching the graveled road;
slamming doors in the distance.

When evening becomes night;
dark cutouts and mountain silhouettes.

The breeze stirs;
rattling waxy leaves, balsam and the
scent of bright rushing water.

I rest my hand on her smooth inner thigh;
laughing, she gathers up her hair.

Walking home through dappled light;
there's peace in our quiet world.

That summer night—nearly the shortest—
needed no sleep from us [sleep never found us].

Butts and Ash [13]

What I miss most is the way she looked at me:
that frank, acute, accepting gaze.

It was the day before Christmas when I drove
her to the airport. One of those lovely dry winter
days so comfortable in the sun, with that tangy
scent of melting snow on the air [like oranges],
and the panoramic view of Front Range jagged
teeth and shimmering snowy Divide.

It was a much sadder scene inside. With little left
to say, we stood mostly in forlorn silence. Then
she boarded her plane and was gone.

Walking back to my car I found myself in the
oddest mood, this crazy sort of tangled up
saudade-like mix of emotions: emptiness, serenity,
melancholy, regret, anticipation, nostalgia, relief, loss.

And if not for the stale smell of her cigarettes how
cozy it might have been to linger there in my car
giving all that a good ponder.

But as it was, just before I backed out I pulled
the ashtray from the dash and held it out at
arm's length upside down to give it a good shake,
and when I looked … nothing but damp asphalt,
cigarette butts, and ash.

There were Christmas decorations everywhere
on the drive home, colorless in the bright
midday sun.

Red, White, and Blue Beach [14]

Living in his camper out at Red, White, and
Blue beach; down where the arroyo widens
out; a hidden vale beneath benchlands of
spikey Brussels sprouts.

We sat in lawn chairs from the thrift store
[plastic webbing], smoking, watching the
endless break. I wondered: during those
big winter swells, didn't the waves break
where we sat?

No, no work, not then, though he'd once
been a gambler: a horseplayer forever down
on his luck. It was chasing winners that
made him so: a loser [one of the track's
hard truths; there are so many].

He had a little Coleman propane cook stove—
his camper's rig—and in the evening,
waiting in golden light for the fog to roll
back in, we had spartan meals chased with
ample Bonny Doon.

I slept in my bag lee side under a fragrant
Coyote Bush [*Baccharis pilularis*: in the sun,
tiny, creamy yellow flowers like buttered
popcorn]. Warm and cozy, but soon
enough bleary mornings of cold gray fog
and the low tide stink of kelp.

In town, he knew everyone. Up and down
Pacific, these friends from other lives, mid-
Sixties refugees, the fabled Haight diaspora: seeds
cast at random over the Santa Cruz Mountains.

But I never broached the subject of his losing
or why he believed he could hide from the
improbable [*that* whatever it is that keeps
us from truly knowing what to expect,
mistakenly believing, of course, we do].

Later, friends said Golden Gate and Bay
Meadows had finally drawn him back; back
to all those calculated risks and probable
humiliations. I thought how heroic; Achilles'
beachy seclusion has gone on long enough.

Though he later moved to Australia. I got a postcard.

Salacious Tavern [15]

Not for me the Salacious Tavern [*salax taberna*] with its
whoring, drinking, and gambling. Certainly not like when
I was a young man making my way down that narrow alley,
through those oaken doors, into that dark interior…

With age comes decorum, or at some point what you used
to do [*all* the time!] grows stale; how we miss the surprises, fear
the slow decline of expectation and satisfaction.

I say whoring, but that's wildly inaccurate. These were, as
I remember them, good times ending in similar nights. The
women, the men, none unlike myself—cool, insouciant,
heedless—there *were* no consequences past noon the next day.

Yes, I do still gamble, though just a bit, and then only within
the safe confines of the pari-mutuel corral where my opponents
are anonymous, summative, and abstract, but it's just as joyful
to beat the crowd as the person who sits across from you.

Drinking? Maybe a little wine [unmixed *Falerian*], or an occasional beer, but never liquor. Not these days. Abuse your body long enough it *will* tell you when to stop. Of course you must first learn to listen, but the passage of time is, if for nothing else [*is* there anything else?], learning.

So no more salacious behavior for me, and not because I fear to act up in public—I could freely walk back through those doors at any time—but because I've outgrown it. You, however, are quite different. No? That's why I've written this little epigram on the repressive roots of neuroticism. I've written it just for you:

> Behavior [salacious, lustful] once public, there free of fear and shame, now finds itself cowering behind closed doors. Well, I suppose you've just forgotten: the repressed [especially the repressed] always expresses itself best where it hurts the most.

Shaft [16]

January Shaft's walkabout Harlem Puck we're watching watch out John Bumpy's crippled newsy's Ray-Bans Isaac wah-wah guitar sex machine right on brother *Wild Thing* is her ringtone she's *not* with Roundtree.

1971 – cat – from the red couch – got a job for you – "A crippled newsy took 'em away from him. I made him give them back." – Hayes – Blaxploitation – The Troggs cover the Wild Ones – she's in New Orleans – Richard.

The Least [17]

The best cast aside,
the worst waits in the queue,
the least presented here today.

Blues Night [18]

Gliding sliding blue night streets,
steeply pitched arroyo bottoms.
In the gloom threaded cones of light,
blue lights blues night,
our last rendezvous.

El Naco [19]

All Mexifornia mourns the loss
this morning to Brazil,
Mexican flags flagging,
much unhappiness at El Naco,
las ficheras y micheladas.

Lucid [20]

Indecisive,
standing in the driveway
under the pepper trees,
crunchy seeds underfoot,
lucid winter light,
a day that
promised options
nudged no decision.

Mulch for My Garden [21]

I've saved only one:
Life is like slapstick, funny until it happens to you.

Otherwise ...

five per page
100 pages
through the shredder
mulch for my garden
an epigrammatic garden of
ghost peppers.*
[*Bhut jolokia; 1,041,427 SHU]

Sense [22]

Reading a text this afternoon, it was just a torrent of words.
Any sense it had drowned in the maelstrom.

The Beach [23]

Sous les pavés la plage.

Parisian graffiti, May '68,
stumbling here to the present
as critical coinage in theoretical exchange,
the value of which,
the meaning of which,
remains ever enigmatic.

Under the pavement, the beach.

I've read:
a wobbly line ...

the drunkard's walk …
flânuer …
Baudelaire …
Benjamin …
a new praxis of aimlessness …
of drifting …
subverting the expression of capital and consumption …
and thought, but where is this beach?

Maybe I'd like to go on holiday.

Desire [24]

ongoing / exsistent / embrace
sensuous / existent / duration
moment …
moment …
moments …
carnality / existence / desire

That Chance [25]

I hold here in my hands all chances.
Even weighted no one knows which will be.
We've always just had to wait.
But I hate wasting time on anticipation.
So … I'll choose indifference.
Why not? It's going to happen anyway.
That chance I'll toss to the wind.
But why am I even thinking about this,
This notion with its ancient pedigree?
It's had a good run, it's seen its day
[and taken up far too much of our time].
No. I refuse [to waste time].

Pleistocene Relic [26]

When I saw the tweet on Osage Orange [*Maclura pomifera*] I asked my brother if they hurt when we threw them at him.

Gnarly little tree with dense wood, green seedpods large like grapefruit but sticky, wrinkled and heavy, a softball fit for the hand. Scientists now wonder [I read] how they've managed to propagate with no megafauna left to consume them [we've killed them all]. This mysterious Pleistocene relic used by frontier farmers for hedges.

But next to that tough little tree was a tall oak, and way up there an enormous wasps' nest, a magnificent paper acropolis they finally succeeding in dislodging [their rocks thrown straight up]. What ensued: a swirling black swarm, the frantic dash to the Plymouth station wagon sitting in a driveway down the block, their safe refuge as angry wasps pinged off the glass, and that one little boy who fell behind [Johnny]. Who knows how many times he took a sting [he was never quite right after that]? Still, his father turned the incident into a script for a B-movie horror flick. [Strange deaths plagued the neighborhood for months: gruesome welts, cries of agony in the night.]

I'm told [by my brother] that Native Americans [First Peoples] used that dense wood for bows [*bois d'arc*].

Forgotten [27]

We had this conversation at his door:

"The one who remembers is the one who leaves. Those
who stay …"
"They forget?"
"By next week."
Then there was our laughter, because, well … it's true.
And then he added this:
"I can't remember all the times I've been forgotten."

I took that as paradoxical.

Emptied Life [28]

solace sought
never found

last drink
late smoke
late night's lament
but spoken—it should be spoken [to whom?]

finally turned out
night streets
to damp streets
lonely streets home

this emptied world
emptied life
late at night
never forgotten [just try]

Overlain [29]

But what *is* under that pavement?

You'd say:
dirt, the sand of urban life paved over with
angular stones, thick, heavy, well-seated,
occasionally prised free to make a political
statement.

Or my preference:
one of those long-buried, fabulous classical
mosaics with tiles more complex than
pixels [how *did* they do that?].

But suppose it's metaphorical:
there's a tear in the social fabric, rent
open, revealing a glimpse of a different life.

Or doused with philosophical swagger:
an anonymous enigmatic epigram [a
Situationist epigram?] plopped into the
rush of history to be flung this way and
that by the dialectic, always with an unsure
[unknown] telos.

But perhaps this would be best:
not under, but *overlain* [washed-up] on this
pavement, a beach.

Nadir [30]

decay
leaves falling
fallen
volatile terpenes and isoprenoids
a deep plunge into olfactory memory
autumn's melancholy harvest

darkening days
a cut of twilight
a lingering summation

but lurking there beneath notice
winter's austere scent
an uncanny stillness

again, nadir

I'm at a Loss Here [31]

Rain last night
[third storm this season]
and raining still.

When I was up,
in reflected light
my black street glistened.

But it struck me,
this thought:
it glistened,
it just glistened,
and not glistened *like a* …
it—just—glistened.

Glistening,
my black glistening street.

Have you seen that,
your glistening black street?

I'm at a loss here:
is there something more I should say?
Anything more I *could* say?

Stray Dogs [32]

he had a look
a look to him
[think film noir sociopath]
like when you met him
introduced by a friend
there was this chill pause
as it all dropped away
that intersubjective world
of implicit normalcy and civility
those assumed givens of social life
because he didn't live there
he didn't even have the address
so you were just sort of there
in that stricken moment
he's looking at you
expressionless eyes
angular smile
and you have this crazy
existential epiphany
for the first time you see
just how foolish
your assumptions
about the world and your place

in it truly are
it was massively chilling

although there were times I would
have liked to borrow that look

once, looking for another
young woman he came in
to where I was working
and said this to me:
"Bro' if you ever need anything
don't hesitate to ask.
You know, *any thing*."

tempting offer of a blunt favor
when people just refuse to listen

it scared me
a dark shape by my car
after midnight
after work
and just as I reach for my keys
tightly gripped to rake
someone's face
he speaks
marooned [by some woman]
he's walked down here to wait
knew I'd be along
asking for a lift home
I light a cigarette
offer him one
bruised face in the flaring light
laughing, exhaling, sardonic smile
that chills me

on the pavement

scattered grains of white rice
a shred of aluminum foil
strange to remember now
it's the mind clarifying dread
the heightened stark awareness
of *this* particular here and now
that fixes memory's odd details
but choices are made
actions committed to
crowding the hope that nothing
comes from *this* moment

well … stray dogs always take to me
not that I go out of my way to befriend them

Empty Pockets [33]

It was New Year's Eve. They were marching across a
windswept plain, long lines of men and women in the
numbing cold. Heavy loden coats, tattered orange
banners, I watched for as long as I could but finally
had to turn away to seek warming shelter.

Dawn was gray and bleak. Despite the timid sun and
howling winds I hurried back to the crest of the hill
but now they were nowhere to be seen, not a single one,
just trackless wilderness with no footsteps to follow.

At the base of the trees were little empty pockets in
the drifting snow.

You could stand with your back to the wind and
lean into it.

There was no sense in thinking about anything but shelter.

I've Got the Blues [34]

It's always been a wonder, a red shifted conundrum.
Stupendous odds. Blue odds. Deep blues odds.
Ultra-odds.

From mere happenstance to rigid causality, but there
in the blue, the mistaken chance/there is no chance; it's
all coming together.

Haphazard but fit, singular and universal, first to last,
now and then; but [still] they were well suited.

Someone said it could only have happened here.
Someone else said it only happened to happen here.

I've got the blues.

Null Sets [35]

Left my mojo in the dojo.
Maybe someone will find it more useful than I did.
He meant with women.
He said mostly he'd been persona non grata,
Which shoved me into universal implications,
Ontological states of *unwelcomed-ness* …
And by then null sets littered the ground:
Women, Being-at-home-ness.
I guess that would be in a trailer park.
The Shady Dell in Bisbee,
But that's hardly a *no-place*,
Though it's a *going-no-where* without a car place.
A *no-go*?
I think that's what he meant:
His life had been mostly *no-go*.

An embodied Zeno's paradox,
Parmenidean stasis,
Which is not going to be very helpful in the dojo.
And null sets?
Let's just scratch that,
Nearly empty was always the way to go.

A Wasted Destination [36]

in a blues key
   El Chapultapec – Davy Byrnes – King Eddy Saloon
a favored darkened bar
   Frolic Room – Bully's North – 100-To-1
El Bar noir
   Whale Bar – Vesuvio – Broken Drum
secured, a snug fit
   Levy's – Chatsubo – Dexter Lake Club
sipping upstream in a peaceful eddy
   Peggy's Hi-Lo – El Naco – Shatter Inn
drink
   The Moon Under Water – Salacious Tavern – Tabard Inn
drank
   The Sink – The Baked Potato – Formosa Café
drunk
   Tonga Hut – Dingo Bar – Gay 90's Bar
to a tapped-out port
   The Farolito – Hotel X – Grasshopper Hill
in a wasted destination

Miðnætur Sól [37]

blue iced angst
blau eis blár ekkert
ísjakanum berg under
hielo azul augustia
night-raced miðnætur sól
Baffin Island sere haze
circle point asunder

Bacterium Rex [38]

fought that war
drowning in lactation
tied up in microbial tape
barred by frictionless borders
bored war
distended mammulation
bacterium rex
fenced by laymen
souk penicillin
pilled with bacon
flotsam jetsam
Mesopotamian hydration
dog sick Tigris puke Euphrates
bartered ziggurats
for palm shaded relaxation

2
....

THE GAMBLER'S TALE

Tout [39]

A rare Hibernian cartomancer, this tarot reading tout;
doubts at bay, we'll bet the gambler's tale today.

Lucky [40]

A lucky shrift-shirted Mitteleuropean Vegas poker player;
a *digitus minimus manus* silver thimbled prayer.

Venus Throw [41]

The Venus throw, a lucky stroke, chokehold on fate, but fate
went broke.

Improbable [42]

Bayesian shots in the dark, improbable probables, intended
possible impossibles.

Prognosticator [43]

Viscera splattered Etruscan haruspex, liver reading Babylonian
prognosticator, organic verities entail, entrails authenticator.

Smoking Bolides [44]

Reading numerological intaglios on clacking turtle shells,
interpreting smoking bolides above ancient tells.

Dog Star [45]

Learned Venusian mathematicians in diluvian cuneiform
wedges, measuring the morning star's shadow on
Dog Star temple ledges.

Star Speckled [46]

Unbroken horizon, heaven's star speckled dome,
flooded landscape, Uruk, Gilgamesh's home.

Days of mismatched lunar twins, days of bitter strife,
beneath a wave, above a wave, begins a better life.

Constellated Sky [47]

Lost child of an occluded universe, wayfaring navigator of a
constellated sky, portent reading neophyte the gods perennially
deny.

3
....

POETIC QUALIA

Splatter [48]

Lightning stroke drizzle pitch splatter fest
Blues harp B flat tango

Rondo [49]

Bacterium delirium lightshow no show
Bongo drum rondo respondo

Facile [50]

Pompous prolix posturing picnicker
Facile linguistic bombs away bingo

Bitstream [51]

Deafening aural bitstream tsunami
Poetic tequila and rhyme lingo

Day-Glow [52]

Homeward bound time nibbling wage slaves
Skittery day-glow limbo

Endgame [53]

Dangerously robotic mismanaged autoclaves
Cursory endgame timeshare pachinko

Locoweed [54]

Flourishing clandestine cannabis moonglow
Over fertilized locoweed home grow

Qualia [55]

Poetic qualia building block shockwave
Endless heaving-ho blindsiding slideshow

Stick Men [56]

Maginot blockchain overkill winter camp
First stick men forest goes pinko

Au Go-Go [57]

Raging antique strip-teasing blond sumo
Bimbo nights forever au go-go

Chef's Special [58]

Keto dieters eat mumbo jumbo
Crunchy today's chef's special Oreo gumbo

Con Verso [59]

Last chance shambolic letterpress quarto
Turning the page con verso

Dojo [60]

Secret rites of spring green dojo
You too be someday judo mojo

Odyssey [61]

Earth's last man saddest hobo
Endless odyssey seizing wrong topo

Lucky Striking [62]

Ex-o smoking Kent lit cigarillo
Lucky Striking Chesterfield Pall Mall's peccadillo

Blotto [63]

Evanescent chattering bunghole
Ass-bouncing Jägermeisteringly blotto

Haboob [64]

Heat stroke haboob dust fest shakedown
The original Bob lub-jobbed boho

Cumulo-Nimbo [65]

Speedo-magneto cumulo-nimbo gelatto
Play dough chilled jaydo sky high lotto

Semiosis [66]

Blinding semiosis whiteout hurricano
Signage ablating snow shod custom Bullitt resto

Merry Mayhem [67]

Yellow-jacketed snug fitting logo
Politically French merry mayhem mambo

Catullus [68]

Holding court at the *salax taberna* [Salacious Tavern] …

Catullus mixing metaphors with Neo
Dying much too young like James Dean-o

4
....

THE ORDER IN WHICH
THEY CAME - 2

Refugio [69]

Disdainful refugee chatter of lives
     lost to paradiso.
Sitting in the lounge anxiously
     marking time at Hollywood's
Hotel Abyss refugio.

La Nuit Américaine [70]

It's like day for night black and white [*la nuit américaine*].

We're standing
on the outside of a curve when a white car flashes past.

From inside the car
we catch a quick glimpse of a woman [we think it's a
woman] throwing what appears to be a hammer [but
maybe it's a length of pipe] at us.

I'm driving and
my side window shatters, showering me with innumerable
tiny angular bits of [green] glass I sweep from the dash
with my arm [the dash is red metal].

We watch
from the curve as the car slows, swerves, then accelerates.
It has tail fins.

Peligroso! [71]

What only looks like perpetual motion as I drive down your
well-travelled highways … where I'm likely to see: careening
crunching twisted age restricted pile-ups; sideswiped blindsided
rites of passage crash fests; rear-ended fender bending air bag
deploying just in time demo derbies; misjudged apex looping
mythic skid rides; dead end no way out cul-de-sac fear griped
speed runs to nowhere; and it's true, there are moments when
it's most like bumper cars to infinity: trapped in ozone infused
sparking arcing no exit lit roundabouts.

Peligroso! You've missed the warning signage in the mist.
Having always driven too fast, this is my seventieth moving
violation.

Waylaid By The Scent Of Jasmine [72]

We, V and I, were over at Carmine's seated near the front at
our favorite table when this attractive couple came in, and as
they passed I caught a whiff of jasmine [Jean Patou?]. It was
not unlike catching the intoxicating scent of a tropical island
while still miles at sea.

"The jasmine?" V asked. I nodded. "Makes me feel like that
young man in Paris."

She said every act of love is a betrayal, that love swings too
close to pity, is exhausting, unsustainable, the self's most
cherished delusion. I challenged her: but isn't love less an act
than a state of being? She smoked [Gitanes]. She refused to
answer. I thought, well, she's just being French. You know
how they just seem to dance? So I pushed. Pushing until I

ran aground on Cartesian bedrock: that typical mix of full-on doubt and unshakeable certitude. Yes, it is a volatile mix; probably time to queue up the worldly melodrama.

She wept. She told me she was unable to love herself, an impossible love none dared follow. "And which self would that be?" I asked, thinking I can play this game. "You think that makes a difference? This tedious march, this endless charade inhabiting empty personae?" She was now very angry. "So which would you have me be? This woman you would love, because I'll never be her for you." I struggled to speak, but I lacked the subtly, the wit, my words frozen, breaking free to shatter on the ground forever unable to move her beyond mere acts of love or to seduce her into any state other than ratiocination.

V listened, she took it all in, then laughed. "You Stewart boys are so melodramatic." I smiled. We were. "Come on," she said, and we clinked our wine glasses to truth.

It's a fact [and maybe even true] that as you go along in life you can't help but gather up a few useful snippets of understanding [and these too are true?], such as it's all connected, or, if it's ironic then it's much more likely to occur. And then there's this one, jasmine scented for quick recall: there are no right decisions, only panicked reactions. Yes, troubling, but not to worry, it's just something I picked up over in Paris.

Hemp Years [73]

The big surprise is you don't feel the years. Drug around like thick hemp rope tangled at your feet. There's no stepping aside. But those aren't just years, they're consequences.

Enigma [74]

Nothing lasts.
Experience is discrete, monad like.
Life is a zero-sum game.
Nothing is like anything else.
It's too late to be an enigma.

Luminous Ribbons [75]

An angry night filled with twisted darkness, deluge,
incessant lightning, great rips of thunder.

A frigid dawn, the sun a pale ghost in an icy sky of
fitful sparkling crystals.

Dead leaves, burnt orange on rain slicked black rock.

A chilling breeze sidles through the trees.

Mid-afternoon, clearing skies and crisp shadows.

Dusk lit luminous noctilucent clouds, cold mesospheric
lustrous ribbons.

Tiny blue lights, soft dancing nighttime blue shadows,
the Milky Way strung in a mesquite.

Mare Serenitatis [76]

There's clanging rain on the roof but the thunder has ceased.
For the moment it seems the busy world has forgotten me. I
sail the *Mare Serenitatis.*

Dark Pines [77]

Damp night
Deep stillness
An owl speaks from the dark pines

Mima Meadow [78]

In the fog unseen
El Coyote sings to me
across the mima meadow

Banana Slug [79]

It rained heavily all night. In the morning the oaks were
still dripping as I ran the trail down to the redwoods in
Wilder Gulch. It was along there I saw a banana slug in
the duff, and when it was still there upon my return I
stopped to move it to safer ground. But it was lifeless,
though still yellow like a banana. Slick, no bigger than
my index finger.

Alone [80]

Another time I stumbled upon an abandoned encampment
while bushwhacking deep in the woods. A bicycle, some
clothes, and an enormous bath towel emblazoned with the
majestic head of a lion tightly stretched out between the
limbs of a redwood. Like this: coming around the tree he
was already there staring at me, and startled, I froze, though
soon I saw we were alone. Deep-in-the-still-forest alone. I
may have been the last to see him.

Defiled [81]

down in the dark gulch
hidden among the trees
a small concrete dam
a laddered flume for redwoods
ancient trees fueling lime kilns
cement to rebuild quake busted
wanton San Francisco
but one still stood where I
found it one morning
tucked-in deep in a cleft
a mysterious presence in
a defiled landscape

Gilets Jaunes [82]

My imaginary interlocutor is a *gilets jaunes*. It's not just
me not being extreme, being ever reasonable, it's more like
there's no middle ground with her. No, really, see for yourself,
you won't find any. Maybe this means I'll have to live with
these endless questions and emendations.

But that's a life lived in the rubble, surviving like a stray dog
in the ruined Eurasian megalopoli after the Three Dragons
War. Know this: stray dogs do what they have to, they'll eat
anything and in time they'll go feral, devolving back in nature
to match their alpha predator predecessors, the wolf in them
ascendant. Does she really want that?

Foraging for food, I found the dumpsters at Petit Trois. She
told me that made her proud, that I could live on the street
paw to mouth. You know how rich people always leave so
much behind? Table scraps? But with no seat at their table
we see how they waste; their foolish endgame? Perhaps, but

I think she's overplayed her hand.

What? Stray Dog pizza is now on the menu at Mozza's? But it's vegan. Such fucking bad luck. I'd growl if it weren't so ironic. But all along my yellow jacket said just expect it. So, yeah, down, but still counting to ten in Los Angeles. Hardly out of it yet. A smiling dog foraging in the rubble: freed of want, freed of need, free of it all.

Le Carambolage [83]

I tried to quiz her when fame finally found me …

I wondered how it made her feel when they brought the 405 to a standstill in honor of my birthday. Or if she was proud of me when they moved my rally from the Staples Center to the Coliseum. But mostly I wanted to know what she thought about that new martini they'd named after me at Musso and Frank. *Le Carambolage*? But I had to bark to get her attention.

Mean Nothing [84]

I want to write something that evokes nothing
    in the reader;
like non-representational art; like an "object" with no
intentional entanglements; words that just are with no
significant connotations; the barest denotations. Not
nonsense;
nonsense
    means at least that,
but words so transparent as to not
    mean anything:
as to mean nothing.

Counterfactuals [85]

Awake all night trapped in a thicket of counterfactuals:
obsessing, pondering old choices, lives I do not live. It's
true some beckoned, but others I hardly noticed, and now,
well … nothing's that obvious.

Go Back [86]

I caught her reminiscing about the summer of 1965.
    She was fourteen.
    That was today.

She never mentioned the summer of 1960.
    She was ten.
    That was 1965.
    I should have asked.

I knew a bit about her summer of 1967.
    She was seventeen.
    But in 1968 it just slipped past me.

I know we'd all like to go back, but for different reasons.

The Ides [87]

It's the middle of March, the Ides, and I'm ready to shed this
winter. Soon, perhaps even tomorrow, it will just fall away
and I'll no longer care. March, this most rational month:
nature all neat and tidy before things again get fussy. But
tomorrow I'll wonder how tyrannicide got lodged in such a
clear-sighted month. I'll think about this as I walk, when it
will seem absurd.

Variegated Sage [88]

Out of nowhere it was suddenly in the seventies today.
Yesterday winter, today spring. It's like this every year,
this brief burst of early summer; a good time to get a jump
on cold rainy spring weather.

In the past I've used this time to put down golden hued
flagstone under the drain spout by the garage, heap deep
red mulch around my trees and shrubs, and rake dead
leaves from under my Tricolor and Variegated sage [*Salvia
Officinalis*].

Miss this opportunity and you'll feel regret, like the year
the cold dreary wetness didn't break again until the Fourth
of July weekend when summer finally stepped forth in a
whiteout balmy haze.

Like nature, be opportunistic.

Lucky Puck [89]

Starlit nights, a patterned existence, this is where my cat really
thrives, and you've got to admit where it counts his cognitive
equipment is first rate. No, he's not much troubled by your
Ding an sich.

Nocturnes [90]

It's a strange church she serves, not golden and purple,
domed and spired, but just as empty.

But her wan faith demands blood red devotion; her failures
hers and absolute; the sacrament her loss of certain anonymity.

Her pallid skin, the way she stumbles in the morning, that she coughs when she runs, none of this is unknown.

They will always know where she is.

I chased this all night over golden fields of wheat stubble. It's stiff, spikey, it's not hard to stumble. I've been here before, these nocturnes, this seer-scape. I'm expecting to find her near, serene.

I will always know where she is.

Link Wray [91]

Sure-handed
        Muddy Waters
  Who I dreamt about the night he died
  Not that I'd known until the next morning
         Slide guitar
Private lessons
His sole appearance on my stage

Equally sure-handed
        Link Wray
  In my dreams this morning when I woke
  But already dead 14 years
          Blistering, scorching, rumbling
Power cords
         This massively complicated bit
Way up the fretboard that had the band jumping
And whooping off camera
         I dreamt him forever young and
Slim, Native American [THE] rebel still awaiting
His due off my stage

Sputnik [92]

Was that small silvery diode with the clear plastic cap and thread like black wires really thrust deep into her thigh? I'm terrorized. It's like a spiky little Sputnik. I see my back. It's dotted with unctuous knobby red welts. I recall Laika and the Cosmonauts. I hear *Floating*. That steady beat. I think poor little dog, now we're all wired like you.

The Last Nightcap [93]

One looks for the epic moments: By 549 AD there wasn't much left of Rome. It was then, under Totila, King of the Ostrogoths, that the last chariot races were held in the Circus Maximus. When we were kids we used to say this is where I came in, then stand and leave the theatre.

Putting Words On Clay [94]

Of this I've read: Spoken of by Berossos in his *Babyloniaca*, the fish-bodied human-headed monster Oannes emerging from the Persian Gulf at the dawn of time to teach humans the skills necessary for writing and mathematics.

Or this more prosaic explanation from *Enmerkar and the Lord of Aratta*:

Because the messenger's mouth was too heavy, and he could not repeat it,
   The lord of Kulab (Enmerkar) patted some clay and put the words on it as on a tablet.
   Before that day, there had been no putting words on clay;
   But now, when the sun rose on that day—so it was!:
   The lord of Kulab had put words as on a tablet—so it was!

Charpin says: "The spoken word held in the clay ... oral discourse fixed on a support." Yes, but it's mouth heavy bookkeeping that was the origin of writing. Impressed edged—wedged cuneiform. After that, it was "a long time before anyone read for pleasure."

[Dominique Charpin: *Reading and Writing in Babylon*]

Baked Text [95]

Divination's the key,
  to foretell the future the desire.
        Oneiromancy
        Heptomancy
        Astrology
        Cleromancy
        Auspicious omens
Wet clay and a reed calamus.
  Perhaps we'll find a baked text.
  Perhaps we'll learn the art of living
  with no surprises.

Chicxulub [96]

Chicxulub, that's in Mayan Yucatan, but go during the dry season. Being wise, she said here's my KT boundary, here's my before and after, my paradise to anything but; this stark cleaving of a life, cratered life, such fierce ejecta, the all consuming fires, and how long was it before she saw the sun again? Chicxulub, she never saw it coming; his oppressive shadow, though there's still a man in her life. If you get there try a Ceiba, a local brew named after the sacred Ceiba tree, which are quite handsome.

Magic [97]

The humid air is heavy, with a surprising closeness.

With no stirring breeze time hangs like mist among the trees.

>Summer days when nothing happens;
>no afternoon longer, no twilight deeper.

But when night falls we wait for magic under the walnut trees.

We reach the cracked undulating concrete pavement at the base of the hill.

>It's a hazy tableau of darkest greens and lazy nighttime shadows.

Muffled sounds. Only the thrumming seams seem near.

But rising up, rolling down, we sight a distant bus.

>Its squat labors and large panes of glass, the light yellowed as it pushes through the viscous air.

It glides past. The whoosh jostles us like leaves in the gutter.

But we saw her, the sole passenger standing by the driver.

>I smell acrid diesel in its wake. I feel a nameless emptiness as I step back into the shadows. My limbs fill with achy longing.

Of course it's all magic.

Even More Magical [98]

Though the next we target with bottle rockets.

> Sticks broken in two, lit, sent hounding down the
> street, fizzling trajectories, sparking gold, popping
> as they go off. The one that finds its target makes
> a small thunk when it strikes.

Whooping with laughter, we retreat up the hill to the
walnut grove.

Just Chill [99]

My neck's sweaty, my t-shirt damp.
Chasing nighttime thoughts, my youthful mind skitters.
Which is it to be, playfully serious or seriously playful?
Quipping melancholia or holy fool?

Muggy still, but cooling breezes spring a delicious chill.
It's into this space I've wandered.
I will say this: it's the heat you feel, but the chill is for
Thinking it through.

The Worm in the Apple [100]

I wandered that property as a young boy.

> Over to what once had been a putting green,
> though I never saw any putting. Out to the
> abandoned grape trellises on a slope with sunny
> western exposure. To the far southwestern corner
> of the property where I stumbled upon the
> overgrown ruin of a large circular stone fountain
> filled with a stalky thicket of pale orange irises.

I had my landmarks.

> West, the regal tulip tree, to the back, the massive mulberry whose fruit stained the concrete walk purple. The lithe pine by the front porch, its bare inner limbs a secret ladder up a darkly lit green tube. The gaping open-mouthed cistern near the bottom of the hill by the avenue: rough stonework, mossy green, fifteen feet deep, eight across, mute and compelling. The walnut grove where we took shelter: the bitter smell of rubbery green walnuts rubbed on concrete, tannic green stains, small nuts at their core.

Even though we were up on the bluff among the trees

> the breeze often carried the sickly sweet scent of meat packing plants and the hydrocarbon smog generated by the heavy industry down in the river bottoms. Also there the Santa Fe railway yards. On still nights I'd hear the shuddering impacts, the clanks and straining diesel engines, the blatting harmonic train horns. An aural Fata Morgana: oddly near but distant sounds piercing the voluminous silence

And yet in the midst of all this was abandonment.

> At first familial, left in someone else's care, the banging screen door, in flight, the unanswered plea, the midday walk to an empty hollowed out place where I found not only that I stood alone but apart. Even now I find myself standing there, though that property is long gone.

But we might prefer this more generic assessment.

> Mere child wandering an enchanted world, the embodiment of a romantic, narcissistic Jungian archetype: incipient *Hero*, his coming of age, the discovery of a personal identity, his forging labors to become who he will be.

Yes, I know, I might have been better off as the *Trickster*.

Never Enough [101]

Longing for nothing in particular.
It's just the carnality of being.
Deeply lustful, but it's never enough.
There will never be enough.

Twice The Telltale Spark [102]

A firefly hovers in the stillness
   among the lilac bushes,
the air sweet with the scent
   of purple flowers.
Then here … a blip of bright yellow.
Guess where it blinks next.

> lilac bushes
> purple scented stillness
> sparking firefly
>
> … where …

Prep. Space Time [103]

under behind
inside without
outside within
beside between
near beyond
around across
along toward
down below beneath
up over above
past next
after before
till since
until following
prior pending
circa nigh
ere while
like ... during

Ubi Sunt: Two Passes [104]

First Pass:
Sunset comes a little earlier without daylight savings time, but it's still on the wrong side of one hundred degrees.

I circle the block in my Alfa. I find a nice spot to park next to three lacy palo verdes.

There's a rusty low iron gate. I walk along the side of the white stucco building to the entrance. A swamp cooler streaks the widows with dripping condensation. It's a damp cold shock when I step in from the heat.

It's El Molino carryout. My order is taken at a shiny white counter much like the one at my neighborhood butcher's. Since there's no indoor seating I stand off to one side. I'm not waiting outside.

My order's ready. Two green corn tamales smothered in tart green tomatillo chili, a side of pinto beans sprinkled with chunky white cotija cheese, and a cold Pacifico.

Outdoor seating is functional, minimal; several battered picnic tables and an array of secondhand pool and patio furniture scattered about on a few squares of white concrete and a rock hard lawn edged by thirty-foot oleanders.

I choose a sadly distressed round poolside table ringed by turquoise plastic folding chairs. Sitting up close to the oleanders I feel the cooling whisper of a breeze.

I can smell my food, their cooking, the moisture from the flooded yards down the street, sweet nearby acacia, and that dusty, hot end-of-the-day desert scent.

My friend says they forget the chips. I say be sure to get more salsa.

Beer in hand, I lean back in my plastic chair. The grass is lumpy and uneven and the chair tips awkwardly to one side.

I'm surprised to see so many people here on such a hot evening.

I watch V walking towards me, a basket of chips in one hand, several small paper cups of salsa in the other. When I try some I'm not surprised to find it's hot and smoky. Her favorite.

I haven't been with her in some time. She talks about work, her trips. We have common friends, fewer common interests, but this was always one of her favorite places.

When we're done I carry the aluminum carryout containers and white plastic utensils over to the trash. But V wants another beer so I step inside for two Bohemias.

She's in a good mood. We laugh. She teases me. For once we've set it all aside.

When we leave the bottles and plastic basket are set on the ledge above the trash barrels, then it's out through the iron gate and up the street to the car. We linger there with the doors open, in no rush to leave the soothing moist air rising from the bermed yards.

I drive. It's getting cooler, darker, dark enough to see Venus. I glance at V. I wonder if she's spending the night.

Second Pass:
Memory's lamenting supplicant,
trapped in time-shifted diurnal cycles
of night struggles and days well spent.

Seasonal, biweekly flooding of the berm,
a fertile age, the Golden Age, El Don the
Juan tilting at his El Molino.

The stage, fixed with El Saguaro Motel relics,
is majestically curtained by salmon flowered
oleander. La mesa, con chili Pacifico tomatillo
y masa harina pinto cotija.

It's a charming tableaux set for smooth talk
and salsa picante. And she's in a mood,
perhaps it's even a proper mood. But in
this theatre it's always a melodrama: staged,
stale dialogue, a repetitious venue for clichéd
players with tamed passions.

Tonight it will be *Venus Ascendant in the House
of Ripened Corn*.

Eros 2019 [105]

Pull down your pants with confidence
Going LIMP too often? Watch this …
"Holy grail" of men's bedroom performance discovered in
	ancient jungle
Why you grandfather's stiffy was better than yours
Aztec remedy for 'hard as rock' performances at any age…
Problems getting hard? Watch THIS….
Think you can't perform because you're too old? Think again!
Can men have a "second" sexual prime?
Secret Plague KILLS your erections (Doctor Verified)
This Strange Brew Gets Her More Attracted To You
Hijack Her Sexual Brain With THIS
Say THIS To Make Her Chase You
This video will show you how to turn on any woman
	INSTANTLY
Ted Talk On How To Fuck any Woman !!!
Say These 13 Words And She'll Chase You Into Bed

So many offers.
Pants down, Eros paces in his panic mode.
That's the new Eros, no one knows what became of
	the elder one.
Plagues of rampaging tumescence, those too sad
	limp members who've lost their way.
Well, the old guy took all his secrets with him.
The rigid discipline of those lustful priapic herms,
	parading phallic phalanxes …
	but off to the ancient jungle?
And Her?
Boy, has she become TED talk difficult.
The crux of the issue is, once won, Her attention
	turns to an iffy stiffy.
Where's your penis envy now?

Ex Nihilo [106]

I believe I've emptied my head.

It takes a long time
to find that empty room.

To empty it.
To see it empty.

Now, out of everything,
from out of nothing,
ex nihilo.

Now, Everything Out [107]

identity, privilege, oppression, inclusion, monetized everyday
selfhood, rules of thumb, rarefied intellects, louche gamblers, a
dazzling potpourri of sensibilities and avidities, comically
tendentious, quid pro quos, drunken brawls, cave art, burial
complexes, the ephemeral taste of analog nirvana, melting
glaciers, to improvise, compress, contrive, tedious, samey,
sedative, blankness, insolvent, banned, chicanery, unasked
questions, incomprehensible Ph.D.'s, triumphant calamity,
darker forces, mystical shaman, surreptitious, subtle, woeful,
archetypal creative obsessive, lumpers and splitters, higher
plane, predictability, the cognitive division of labor, learning
the art of the scribe, digital minimalists, the social organization
of inquiry, a dirty limerick, bleak hilarity, Latin, canonization,
long eclipsed, having a moment, afterlives, galvanic energy,
imaginative possession through language, ex-votos, an
infatuation with the ephemeral, a hunger for the eternal, the
quest for immortality, chuffing puffery, modernist, pulp,
troubadour, songwriter, poet, writing about food, music,
perfume, dubious origin, greed, dark arts, dark prophet,

unnerved totalitarianism, life hacks, doing nothing, digital-detox, profoundly benighted, physical carapaces, equivalent souls, mocks, belittles, futile, catchphrase, literary hangout, intellectual promiscuity, drink, gossip, anxiety, neurosis, venereal disease, unrepentant Nazi, rehabilitation, an eruption of irrational violence, slow drivers, slow internet, slow grocery lines, Celticization, secrets from the antediluvian age, telepathic snails, oversensitive souls, unbearable tedium of lyric poetry, oversaturated, monochromatic, period of piety, connoisseur of discomfort, fearful conformity, intimacy, digital chastity belts, age of feelings, exemplars of irrationality, exemplars of hyperrationality, sweet reason, devoid of value, personal pain, love life, aviophobe, from the real to the ideal, digital humanities, the monetization of attention, cyanotype, shoddy logic, bad math, slowly dying of hunger, quotidian horniness, tedious confusion, relevance, to comfort, to seduce, to pander, nude portraits, tinted, pet names, dinosaur extinction, heedless universalism, awkward disasters, lucid writing, bold, scholarly, criticized, refuted, enduring, cant, sophistry, anti-establishment activism, plagued with anomie and nihilism, *Dialectic of Enlightenment*, in strange sun-kissed exile, Alan fitz Flaad, a handful of begats, handmaid of consumerism, a lit match, pedantic professor, nit, tango-dancing flirt, lekking, dotty performance artist, turned to drink, *The Second Sex*, peculiarly unappetizing Texan lad, exotic thrills in distant lands, handmaiden to sadism and psychopathic violence, hatred of beauty and worship of machines, the fourth wall, the continual thrum of pixel traffic, minimalism, apotropaic inscriptions, beehive or a pine cone

And there,
uncluttered like a defragged disk,
an empiricist's blank slate,
with just a bit of dust still left on the floor.

Plink Bong [108]

plink plop plunk
ring rang rung
ting tang tong
bing bang bong

plunk rung tong bong
plop rang tang bang
plink ring ting bing

plink plunk
ring rung
ting tong
bing bong

plop plunk
rang rung
tang tong
bang bong

plink: there's an algorithm in here somewhere
plop: calculate the number of possible combinations
plunk: do the math

1-1 4-3 [109]

1-1 1-2 1-3
2-1 2-2 2-3
3-1 3-2 3-3
4-1 4-2 4-3

1-3 2-3 3-3 4-3
1-2 2-2 3-2 4-2
1-1 2-1 3-1 4-1

1-1 1-3
2-1 2-3
3-1 3-3
4-1 4-3

1-2 1-3
2-2 2-3
3-2 3-3
4-2 4-3

3-2 4-2 4-3 3-3
keyed to tang bang bong tong
in cryptographic verse

Sumerian Moment [110]

Though firmly lodged in the city's knotted gut
we enjoyed a quiet night. How rare. No hovering
helicopters, no warbling sirens.

It was the last weekend in April and there was a
comforting marine layer that night which chose to
hang around until mid-afternoon.

But mostly my sleep was fitful, which is how, near
dawn, I came to be monitoring the dim shapes
across the cul-de-sac as they slowly resolved
themselves into towering jacaranda.

And no, I don't think this is foolish, how I have these
recurrent troubling worries about what else might
step free of that dim light.

For we exist in the midst of wildness. Wander off
in the wrong moment and you might find yourself
face-to-face with the uncanny.

Like once when I was deep into the night out in
the wilds below Rocky Flats grinding up a long
grade in my red '58 VW and the sweep of my
headlights revealed a creature whose human body
sported a sleekly silver-haired alpaca head.

At first too startled to stop and then too amazed
not to turn back, but of course it was gone. And
although I laughed about it later, at the time it felt
like I'd just taken a huge risk. My wide-eyed
wanderer forever in thrall to his need to know.

So unaware then, certainly, though not so now,
now my jaded wanderer is tempted to say it was
a Sumerian moment, or my Sumerian moment,
that time I was so unprepared to receive the demi-
god's message.

Well, fuck that.

Now I lay awake in my bed at night listening for
the rhythmic whop-whop-whop of the police
helicopters tracking felons across my neighborhood.

Sometimes their spotlights hit my bedroom and I
wonder if they can see me in here. I'd be staring
up at them. They might find *that* uncanny, seeing
my silvery upturned face in the middle of the night.

Rocky Night In Flanders [111]

Awoke at 2 a.m. to watch Paris-Roubaix in bed on
my iPhone, my daft night proving as bumpy as
Flemish cobbles.

Nothing Upstairs [112]

When he retired it
took him more than a year
to remove all that junk
from his attic.

But once he'd cleared it
out he found it hard to
come up with anything new
to replace it.

Ironic. Disconcerting.
His booming big empty echo.

Herzog Owes Me [113]

Herzog owes me, publishing my books under his name. So I
flew to Germany. I was going to confront him during his talk
at the Frankfurter Buchmesse. But the Springer reps shut me
down.   Hustling me out of the room, trying to convince
security to call the polizei. He, the grandee, never even looked
my way. But he knows. I dreamt that. Later, sort of awake, I
added a few details that amused me.

Self-Domesticated [114]

We're domesticates,
like dogs, pigs, sheep, and goats.
Less hormonal spark,
smaller teeth, smaller brains,
no longer feral.
That's why I prefer
my little tabby cat
who's still a bit wild.
No need to be drunk
to get his yowl at the moon.

A Signal in the Data [115]

Drowning in conformity, I picked up a signal in
the data: the freedom of being down and out.
A freedom I'd somehow missed even when I
was down and out. But I suppose I'd struggled
too much to keep what little was left. Now I'd
gladly walk away empty-handed, thankful for
nothing.

And this signal, it is faint, easily overlooked in the
buzz, even near drowning one might fail to notice.
Still, you're already in the water …

No, I do laugh at all this.
So please, keep treading.

Homogamous Man [116]

My whole life, trapped in homogamy. One right
after another, different yet the same.

Nunc Est Bibendum [117]

I've always been more for drinking for than for drinking against, always more for celebration than threnody.

But then they politicized hedonism, kneecapped the personal with the political, salted self-liberation with social justice demonology.

So I ask you: Who fought for the domination of the night? Remember? That battle took casualties, and freed of collective restraints the bars were overflowing.

Though now I'm more hesitant, fearful of exposure to these latest pathologies of conformity and groupthink.

And noticed, they've brought this woke charge against me: Too much the scion of democratized libertines.

Nunc est bibendum.
No quarrels with that.
Now *is* the time for drinking.

.

5

....

CONCEPTUAL

Homer's Odyssey [118]

Tell me about a complicated man …
The man, Muse—tell me about that resourceful man …
Sing to me of the man, Muse, the man of twists and turns …
Tell me, Muse, about that resourceful hero Odysseus …
Tell me, Muse, of the man of many ways …
This is the story of a man, one who was never at a loss …
Goddess of song, teach me the story of a hero …
Tell me, Muse, the story of that resourceful man …
Tell me, Muse, of that man of many resources …
Tell me, Muse, of that man of many devices …
Tell me, O Muse, of that ingenious hero …
The man for wisdom's various arts renown'd,
Long exercised in woes, O Muse! resound …
[The first line of Homer's *Odyssey*, as translated by …]

In The Money [119]

Rumpus Cat, Over Par, Captivate,
Fast Cotton, Lymebyrd, Twisted Plot,
Kid Koil, Jimmy Chila, Unpossible, Writ Large,
Thermopolis, Silent Alarm, Respect the Hustle,
Dis Smart Cat, Miss Unusual, Donut Girl,
Red Livy, Loco Mango, Old Indian Trick,
Chica La Habana, Going Away Party,
Let Me Go Amigo, Girl Downstairs,
Subic Bay, You're A Goat, Nova,

Rockaway, June Sixth, Vegas Itch,
Call Ended, Catapult, Isotherm,
She'sluckythatway, Double Touch,
Comma Sister, Acceptance, Bombard,
Mongolian Shopper, Angelic, Suspicious Spouse,
Chilled Martini, Lady Beware, Awesometastic, Pirate Flag
[Three days at Santa Anita.]

Trip Notes [120]

Met bid; held gamely
Willingly; not enough
Ducked out; lost rider

No speed
Two wide trip; empty

Found best stride late
Bobbled start; rallied

Drew off; kept to task
Passed tiring rivals
[Trip Notes from *The Daily Racing Form*.]

Gappa Captions [121]

Dramatic music
Somber music
Volcano rumbling
Pleasant music
Upbeat music
Waves sloshing
Glass clinking
Groaning
Radio beeping

Water rumbling
City commotion
Jungle commotion recording
Laughing
Boat horn blowing
Groaning
Ominous music
Rumbling
Rumbling
Rumbling
Glass rattling
Water rushing
Groaning
Yelling
Laughing
Laughing
Rumbling
Dramatic music
Ominous music
Rumbling
Water sloshing
Laughing
Chuckling
Boat horn blowing
Water sloshing
Somber bongo drumming music
Ominous music
Menacing music
Yelling foreign language
Cheering
Chanting foreign language
Exciting bongo music
Volcano rumbling
Exciting bongo music
Laughing

Distant bongo music
People chanting
Exciting bongo music
Birds chirping
Sighing
Birds chirping
Birds squawking
Hissing
Ominous music
Menacing music
Rumbling
People screaming
Rumbling
People chanting
Rumbling
Foreboding music
Groaning
Water trickling
Groaning
Water trickling
Steam hissing
Water trickling
Steam hissing
Rocks tumbling
Rumbling
Cracking
Rumbling
Cracking
Ominous music
Rumbling
Saburo whimpering
Dramatic music
Ominous music
Ominous music
Water trickling

Exciting bongo drum music
Steam hissing
Water dripping
Ominous music
Water rumbling
Gappa growling
Menacing music
Growling
Horn blowing
Explosions rumbling
People screaming
Rumbling
Booming
Growling
Footsteps rumbling
Volcano thundering
Roaring
People yelling
Roaring
Screaming
Growling
Screaming
Roaring
People screaming
Footsteps rumbling
Roaring
People yelling
Grunting
Roaring
Water sloshing
Water splashing
Water sloshing
Dramatic music
Whooshing
Laughing

Pleasant music
Baby Gappa squawking
Baby Gappa squawking
Baby Gappa squawking
Baby Gappa squawking
Man yelling
Baby Gappa squawking
Electrical fizzling
Squealing
Yelling
Squawking
Squawking
Grunting
Water sloshing
Rumbling
Waves bubbling
Beeping
Whooshing
Rumbling
Beeping
Beeping
Whooshing
Waves sloshing
Upbeat music
Singing in foreign language
Buzzing
Waves rumbling
Waves rumbling
Ominous music
Menacing music
People yelling
Roaring
Footsteps splashing
People yelling
Footsteps booming

People screaming
Booming
Gappa roaring
People screaming
Footsteps rumbling
Growling
Roaring
Rumbling
Roaring
Buildings crumbling
Trucks rumbling
Helicopters buzzing
Tanks rumbling
Booming
Footsteps rumbling
Gunshots booming
Growling
Roaring explosions booming
Rapid cannon fire
Roaring
Fire fizzling
Explosions rumbling
Growling
Jet whooshing
Jets whistling
Helicopter whizzing
Gunshots booming
Explosions rumbling
Growling
Booming
Explosions booming
Rapid gunshots firing
Explosions booming
Whooshing
Splash rumbling

Dramatic music
Suspenseful music
Alarming sirens
Somber music
Somber music
Squawking
Dramatic music
Motors rumbling
Water sloshing
Motor buzzing
Motor buzzing
Ominous music
Bubbling
High-pitch whistling
Water sloshing
High-pitch whistling
High-pitch whistling
Water rumbling
Water rumbling
Water rumbling
Missiles whooshing
Explosions booming
Growling
Explosions booming
Growling
Roaring
Gappa screeching
Whooshing
Growling
Explosions booming
Roaring
Wave rumbling
Birds chirping
Instrumental music
Rumbling

People screaming
Water rumbling
Roaring growling
Footsteps rumbling
Electrical fizzling
Growling
Helicopters whizzing
Dramatic music
Dramatic music
Footsteps crunching
Whooshing
Steam hissing
Roaring
Explosions rumbling
Fire crackling
Explosions rumbling
Explosions thundering
Roaring
Helicopters whizzing
Roaring
Explosions thundering
Growling
Fire crackling
Distant rumbling
Growling
Fire rumbling
Helicopter thumping
Pleasant music
Growling
Squawking
Squawking
Explosions thundering
Squawking audio recording
Explosions rumbling
Squawking audio recording

Baby Gappa squawking
Gappa roaring
Footsteps crunching
Growling
Squawking
Pleasant music
Squawking
Pleasant music
Growling
Pleasant music
Pleasant music
Whooshing
Squawking
Gappa whooshing
Growling
Squawking
Whooshing
Dramatic music
Pleasant music
Dramatic music
Exciting music
Upbeat music
Dramatic music
[Captions from *Monster from a Prehistoric Planet // Gappa: the Triphibian Monster*.]

Arts & Letters Daily [122]

Things I might not care about anytime soon:
Obfuscatory jargon
Architectural cynicism
Bad sex writing
Punk poet
A diminution of reading
Depicting conceited men
Bad news wrapped in protein
Age of pith helmets
Afterlife of Nazism
The rise of the pedantic professor
The bitterness of being ignored
Prison-camp lectures on Proust
Doommongering
Surveillance capitalists
When America read
Proletarian literature
A cultural history of fat
Banal ceramics and quasi-porn
The first postmodernist
Being cool
Successful art thief
Continuing uglification
Rampant forgeries
Ideophones
New Puritanism
A silver lining
[Keywords. *Arts & Letters Daily* March 23, 2019]

Affirmative Negative
Non-Committal [123]

Almost certainly
Highly likely
Very good chance
Probable
Likely
We believe
Probably
Better than even
About even
We doubt
Improbable
Unlikely
Probably not
Little chance
Almost no chance
Highly unlikely
Chances are slight
[Kernel Density Estimation]
[*Magic 8-Ball* Estimation]
Yes
Yes-definitely
As I see it, yes
Signs point to yes
It is decidedly so
Without a doubt
It is certain
You may rely on it
Outlook good
Most likely
Outlook not so good
Don't count on it
Very doubtful

My sources say no
My reply is no
Better not tell you now
Cannot predict now
Reply hazy, try again
Concentrate and ask again
Ask again later

6

....

THE ORDER IN WHICH
THEY CAME – 3

Parole [124]

He was asked about his surprises …
little things
leaning in
choices
the will unmoored
swamped
awash

About what he'd done first …
squandered time
stepped forth
stopped waiting
swung the door open
shifted burdens
dreamt a lush now

About what he'd found most difficult …
the words
blank faces
saturated colors
loud noises
numb fears
tomorrow's parties

And all this over breakfast at Corky's, where …
tongue tangled in lingo

newly jacketed
debt free
bill paid
tip covered
he finally spoke

Ultima Thule [125]

I've finally gotten around to reading *Tropic of
Cancer*. It's worn me down, these years
spent saying why put it off any longer?

So I'm not.

And then this morning it struck me that a
longer list of all those other things I'm not
putting off any longer might inspire me not to
[will I finally read *Catcher in the Rye*?].

Not that I'm finding much motivation down
between the covers or in the slender gaps among
my unread volumes.

You know Miller lived down and out for some
time? Which I've always found interesting,
though time served in Big Sur doesn't count,
and those last decades over in Pacific Palisades
… like, where's the authenticity now?

But can't we just say it? So often where we
end up is where we wanted to be all along [I
most often find myself sitting in bars at racetracks;
or did until they tore down Hollywood Park].

I'm saying it.

Now – here's the thing:
lost in the swirling grey sea mists of cold northern
climes [until seen by Pytheas],

until recently unknown, but circling forever about
the sun in solitude way out there in the Kuiper
belt [trans-Neptunian object 2014 MU_{69}],

or close by the Pacific Ocean, a deluxe favored
Westside last port of call [though Miller's was
hardly the only one],

perhaps even sitting here on this red couch
listening to ceaseless honking traffic.

No. Not this last one. But ultimate destinations
are tricky. Many times in many ways a false hand
spins us off course.

Our fate.

Washed up like weathered driftwood on Thule's
barren shores.

Contra A Henry Miller Persona [126]

Is it true that everything comes in due time? Can you really be
the happiest person alive if you have no money, no resources,
and no hopes? What sort of person would answer yes to both
these questions?

The Wise Man [127]

I
The survile surveilled; penned in digital cages.

A conjuror lists your numbers; chipped, GPS'ed in 5G.

Movements known, interests and purchases noted and stored, it's those thoughts you've never expressed you'll hold most dear.

Do *not* Google your dreams.

II
Eschewing the Internet of Things, the wise man secures his fortress with analog warriors off the grid in dumbest domiciles.

In a world threated by EMPs he will have a handy pad of paper and a few pencils to sharpen with his knife.

No doubt he will have already:

>   calculated the exact number of gallons of pure water needed to staunch a millennial thirst,

>   secreted his gallons, canned meats and soups, in formerly abandoned cooling radiation proof atomic bomb shelters,

>   and learned to play acoustic stringed instruments even though he's already procured a dozen Honda portable gas generators.

III
There will be times when the wise man needs to embrace irony and contradiction.

Neurasthene's Love Letter [128]

Neurasthenic Cyburbian youth numbed dumb by
gigabytes of cleverly crafted command messaging.

Lost, deranged in socially mediated incommensurate
phantasmagoric nowheres.

Their wills flaccid from disuse, de-sexed genderless
bodies enfeebled with skyrocketing mutational load,
plummeting sperm count, organs clogged with nano-
plasticizers …

it's past the time to bring on the machines—
your Xbox cocks sheathed in digital prophylaxis.

Better Than Auto-Da-Fé [129]

My auto-fiction is mostly fiction.
I'm hanging on to *my* secrets, they cost
too much to just give away.

It seems I dance most with concealment.
My gallery of auto-personae tightly
holding hands in spinning circles.

Mysteries are singular.
Fiction is plural, the I mythic like the me
you hear in your head.

My confession.
I've never written anything I really meant.
So how's that even possible?

Freud Was Right* [130]

It's midnight.
The world's a slick sheen.
You scurry down a dark street.
Your boot heels slip on wet curbing.
Over your shoulder looming shadows trek brick walls.
Your hands clench in empty pockets.
Then—
The doorway you seek, it's been plastered over and painted
Black.
Breath shallow, you fight the panic.
That's what wakes you.
That's what you're left with.

… a dream is never just a dream.
[* "Dreams are never concerned with trivia." *The Interpretation of Dreams.*
(*Die Traumdeutung.* 1899)]

Triggered [131]

The most potent trigger ever:
    Niagara Falls!

Poor Moe and Larry, now we see it was PTSD:
    slowly I turned … step by step … inch by inch …

These old vaudeville gags are toxic.
No safe space is strong enough to protect us.
Please, Curly, wake up. Try to watch what you say.

It's Not Just Oxytocin [132]

She laughed a nicely calculated laugh when I tried to unbutton her tailored blue blouse. And when I raised my eyebrows a bit to ask oh? she unbuttoned herself.

She always shut her bedroom door even when no one else was there, then spoke to me in a quiet voice. Soon I felt I knew her; now I believe some of my memories are probably hers.

By now it's near pointless to try and untangle the years. Even more so in my ceaseless dreaming. Endlessly tugging those tight blue jeans down over her hips.

But if I had to sort her out I'd say she never met me less than halfway. It would be impossible to shrug off someone so singular, so deeply memorable.

It's Just Oxytocin [133]

I unhappily awake from a dream of her. One leg thrust out to cool me like a radiator from under a pile of winter quilts— which is how I sleep these days—sweltering beneath a dream built of ruthlessly consistent inner logics. It's a rocky road we wander, stumbling back from dream state to waking state. It takes time, like, OK, so this is Thursday June 6th and I'm still a bit logy; please, another crazy dream about her?; just shrug it off; it meant nothing; nothing means nothing; think about the day to come, about something pleasant.

You may have noticed that even though I've fled a dream state we've yet to determine the half-life of a memory. Perhaps another Manhattan Project? They're tracking memory trails in cloud chambers down in the bowls of that lab hidden up in the fragrant piñon by the canyon rim. Oppenheimer breaks the news: just as the Great Pyramid at Giza outlives Khufu so too do your memories outlive you [my Great Pile of Cinderblocks at Los Angeles]. But it gets worse. Those sex-charged moist-between-her-legs memories don't even have half-lives. They're not throwing off *any* radioactive particles. I'm told they're for keeps. Nobel Prizes all around for that bit of news.

As in dreams as in life, when we gaze face to face the other gazes back. We may not want to share more, we may want to share much more, we may even long to be we not you and me. It's the Pile-Up At Erotic Crossroads: colliding head-on persons and bashing bodies. But gray-eyed she stares holes right through me, her blowtorch gaze drills me before I can get near. My personhood burned away as she takes me in; blinded like snow blind; blank blink blinking at solar eclipses; just the sense of touch, penis, fingertips, and tongue.

But if I've safely kept my distance I'll say she's like those beautifully depicted ancient Egyptian women with their big eyes. And often she stands like that, arms akimbo but with her left hand on her hip. I'd like to see more bare shoulder if she would, but if I mention this she'll say she needs more gold jewelry and things that clasp and purple lapis lazuli stoned rings to wear. I understand, in my dreams she glints and shimmers under her white cotton gown like a temple priestess; I stand as transfixed as Boris Karloff's Imhotep staring at his Ankhesenamon.

In other words, I've tried to fix a few memories, tried to grant a bit of immortality in word, with the hope that the blank nothingness of eternity might bend a bit in our favor. But just how capacious is memory? Will there ever be enough to soak up all the intimacies? So far unanswered questions, though I do know there will be no residue; not remembered can't even be forgotten.

The Age of Men [134]

I'd been tracking it forever and
it was close, but I still missed it,
The Age of Men.

But here I am in plenty of time
to catch The Age of Small Central
American Women.

Who gather early in the day under
the red awning at Whole Foods to
assert the new quotidian.

Long black pigtails, coffee and buns;
soon they'll be off to clean the homes
of wealthy Angelenos.

Word Hordes [135]

If I were to collect coins my first acquisition would be one of
those silver Athenian tetradrachms stamped with the image of
gray-eyed Athena's little owl. And if I were a word collector I'd
opt for something equally rare. A lost horde of antique words
found buried in a text*. I'd put them up for auction at
Sotheby's and make a fortune as flush lexicographers outbid
one another.

[*partial list: aisthesis, aletheia, ataraxia, chorismos, doxa, dianoia, eidos,
hyle, hypodoche, hypokeimenon, morphe, noeton, ousia, peras, sophrosyne,
symbebekos, ti esti, tode ti, tyche.]

Eudaimonia [136]

Balanced median, twin excess,
shrieking garbled message exceeded.

Fearful darkened vice-stained stairwell,
lurching virtues soon to flight.

But exhaled sharply, smallest self-masteries
and midnight's calculations measured.

Misfortunes trimmed, negated, an up and
down golden dawn relaxed, equilibrated.

Voided Refusal [137]

A lifelong refusal
To do what others do.

A glorious gap
Paved over with books.

In a secret project
Taken in fiction.

Books *they* read
Unread by me.

Even now with
Scant expectation.

Goodbye *Goodbye Columbus* [138]

Ron tells me you have a very interesting job.
I work in the library.
I've always liked reading.
You must get first crack at the best-sellers.
Sometimes.

After all *they* said, clichés?
As always, expecting more I get less.
Now I'm stymied,
My project mired in questions of art.

Ron tells me you have a very interesting job.
I'm a writer.
I've always liked reading.
You must get first crack at the best-sellers.
Only if I've written one.

Forget That Aide-Mémoire [139]

I've just read a book about famous lost books. Isn't there also one about famous books never written? But mine will be among those we never found the time to write. Or perhaps the books we forget to write: books that only became famous when we finally got around to writing about how we forgot to write them. No, my legacy will be hugely unknown; erased traces and forgotten aides-mémoire. And I'll be famous for *that*.

Words Without End [140]

Reads like more of your rambling
    jejune juvenilia,
the gnomic nostrums of an idiot
    savant,
a monoglot's verbal legerdemain,

your bumptious bro's twee
twiddle-twaddle couched in
   capsizing cadence.

      Forever Should Have
      Gone On Much Longer [141]

Smuggled into the house this evening
like contraband, a remaindered copy
of *A Catcher in the Rye*.

I'd asked for it, but queasy; I was never
that youth who read it, forever that
youth who said no.

This never a book I wanted not to read
more, but then yesterday it got read.

And now I try to see me at sixteen, a
fictive cowardly acquiescence in an alternate
universe where I'm turning the pages.

But other than yesterday's it forever didn't happen.

      … Faith In The Ability of Logos To
      Outlive The Finite Mortals Whose
      Ability To Reason Had Discovered It* [142]

Angry misologist or not, this is exactly the sort of poem that
never gets written,

though typically I'd prefer being more
like logos,
independent
   of anything outside myself,

eternal,
self-grounding,
    my own
cause,

but as poet I'm not seeing much here to work with.
[*Martin Jay. *The Eclipse of Reason*.]

It Was Always You [143]

I see you –
behind my mind's eye

I see you –
when I don't look

I see you –
without excuses

I see *you* –
en tôi ti esti *

I see you –
play a dark game of hide and seek

I see you –
at risk

I see you –
pull aside waxy green leaves

I see *you* –
tode ti **

[*see quiddity; (for) the what you are]
[**see haecceity; (for) the who you are]

Solstitial Poiesis [144]

When tomorrow's rising sun strikes
the keyhole it will mark one full
year—midsummer to midsummer—
of poetic labors.

A bright wink, a celestial milestone,
though I may choose to simply sit
and watch shadows wax and wane.

Then it's a headlong rush from there
down to the dark woods as sooner
nights arrive.

No, there's no stepping aside,
no sitting this one out.

I need to plan for next year.

A Gibberish Tongue [145]

It's seems impossible
not to be pretentious.
Melodramatic. My
words drenched in cant,
every one a cliché. I
wonder if I even have
a voice. I'm tempted
to forge my own words.
Clear words with no
excess meaning: meaning
only, solely, what I
intend. Sharp little
words to pick real

things apart just so,
presenting only those
aspects I want to speak
to. This would be my
language of one. Spoken
into the wind, heard by
none, a gibberish tongue,
the purest language of
irony.

My Words [146]

Your words:
   mushy, overcooked,
   hammers and hooks,
   burdened, freighted,
   assumptive and machinated.

I prefer:
   fresh, now words,
   free range, bolting words,
   exact words,
   slimmest and quick words.

the Superfluous Man [147]

Announced just moments ago, in an attempt to
bring a little life to the dreary world of streamers,
the Superfluous Man and Felix will mount the
newest Twitch poetry channel.

Streamed live every morning from the red couch,
the Superfluous Man will commit poetic practice
as Felix provides his typically topical running
commentary.

Yes, that Felix, the wildly popular lifeblogger
already famous for his pithy Trump bashing and
animal rights crusades.

But the most surprising new Twitch twist has to
be the rehabilitation of the Superfluous Man who,
after the *eroge* scandal of 2016, has been ghosting
YouTube in poetic obscurity.

But a huge breakout is predicted, with massive
corporate sponsorship already in the works [Red Bull!].

the Superfluous Man Redux [148]

the Superfluous Man,
the infamous LMIRL pick-up artist,
is back with his sexually charged poetic imagery.

This time,
 let's leave it solely to the imagination.

So Began June 29th [149]

it was soft and gray
it was dim and soothing
it was neither too early nor too late
it was peaceful and unconfused
it was snug and cossetted
it was low ebb and just beginning
Then I heard sirens and looked at my iPhone
it was 5:20 and just like that early morning

Mid-Night July 4th [150]

They didn't bother me earlier in the evening,
but they made me very nervous when I was
up in the middle of the night …

it was so quiet, otherwise …

distant thumps, soft, dense, resonant, sustained,
some in series, and staccato strings of rumbling
pops …

to me, it sounded like the war.

I tuned the lamp off next to my bed …

I could see dim flashes on the wall.

I'd like to not think about it.

Late Evening July 10th [151]

An endless soporific summer day
of hazy humidity punctuated by a
a cooling late afternoon shower.
We split a bottle of Argentine
Malbec with dinner, then sit on
the back porch in blue canvas
chairs listening to crickets and
faint thunder rolling in across
the high plains. It's going to be
a dark night. Cooling. If my
eyes are quick enough I might
see red sprites dancing in the
mesosphere above the distant
lightening.

And then she speaks. She's changed
her mind. She will stay the weekend.

Startled, I practice silence, noting
how the breeze carries the scent of
wet gravel and damp soil, that the
lights are off in the house and I can
barely see her now sitting beside me.
But when her chair creaks as she
turns to face me I quickly revert
to language, to the spoken tongue
of what gets said around the silence.

"Dawn comes early," I say. "Let's wait it out."

Mindscrape Endgame [152]

BitTorrent poets
    Honing to a fine point.
Clock punching Fordists
    Assembling threaded set pieces.
These mindscraping endgame
    Poets of the swarm.

The Secret of Dreams [153]

To answer your question, of course it's imaginary.

I don't understand. Interpret *what*? Nothing like this
has ever happened to me, not even *in* my dreams.

Oh, I'd remember.

So now I'm puzzled. Aren't you the one who put
together that multi-page checklist of the things we
might expect to see in my dreams?

But I thought you said it's been helpful in your
oneirological research?

Oh, I hear you, but I certainly don't remember
seeing anything like *that* on your checklist.

["Do you suppose that some day a marble tablet will be placed on the house,
inscribed with these words: 'In this house on 24 July 1895, the secret of
dreams was revealed to Dr. Sigm. Freud'? At the moment I see little prospect
of it." Freud. Letter to Wilhelm Fliess. June 12, 1900.] [Revealed, not
discovered?] [The house is gone, but there is a tablet and a bench for the
pilgrims. It's said they often fall asleep. No! That's nothing but a joke I
dreamt. Interpret that as you will.]

7

....

GREEK KOMOIDIA

As I Was Coming From
The Piraeus [154]

As I was coming from the Piraeus, it occurred to me
to philosophize about my troubles and confusion.*

        Philosophize?
        Hadn't occurred to *me*.
        But then I'm not in Greece.
    It's the strolling back to Athens from the Piraeus.
        There's just something about that road.
    Even so, I'm not going to admit to any troubles.
    I can't even imagine what sort of troubles those would
be; that I'd want to philosophize about them.
        But I might philosophize about my confusion.
        That seems useful.
        You know what I most want to say here?
        Right?
Dazed and confused.
        Turn me loose on that, you'll see some philosophizing.

*"As I was coming from the Piraeus ..." From Alexis' comedy, *Phaedrus*, as quoted by one of the diner guests in Athenaeus' multi-volume dialogue, *Deipnosophistai* [*Intellectuals at Dinner*].[1] *The Piraeus* is an allusion to the beginning of Plato's *The Republic,* where Socrates tells us of his walk down to the port of Piraeus with Plato's older brother, Glaucon.[2]

[1]Athenaeus 13.562A:
    As I was coming from the Piraeus, it occurred to me
    to philosophize about my troubles and confusion.
    They seem ignorant to me, in short,

these artists of Eros, when they make images of this god.
It's neither female nor male, nor again
god or human, neither stupid
nor wise, but put together from everywhere,
supporting many forms in one shape.
It has the courage of a man, but a woman's
timidity, the confusion of madness, but the logic
of sense, a beast's violence, but the endurance
of steel, and a divine pride.
And these things—by Athena and the gods!
I don't know exactly what it is, but nonetheless
it's something like this, and I'm close to naming it.

[2]Plato. *The Republic*:
I went down to the Piraeus yesterday with Glaucon, the son of
Ariston, to say a prayer to the goddess, and also because I wanted to
see how they would manage the festival, since they were holding it
for the first time. I thought the procession of the local residents was
beautiful, but the show put on by the Thracians was no less so, in my
view. After we had said our prayer and watched the procession, we
started back toward town. Then Polemarchus, the son of Cephalus,
saw us from a distance as we were hurrying homeward, and told his
slave boy to run and ask us to wait for him. The boy caught hold of
my cloak from behind.

Cratinus* Is Drunk, Again [155]

You'll never create anything brilliant by drinking water.[1]

Holy Apollo, what a flow of verses!
The waters are roaring; his mouth has twelve streams,
The Ilissus River's in his throat. What more to say?
If somebody doesn't stop up his mouth,
he'll flood the whole place with his poetry![2]

> I suppose it's been a constant
> worry, drunk since viticulture,
> it's certainly a cliché with an
> ancient pedigree: the tipsy poet,
> the alcoholic author, the drunken

> playwright. But there are other
> entrenched clichés here to see,
> also with ancient pedigree.

Hermes: What of the wise Cratinus? Is he alive?
Trygaeus: He died, when the Spartans invaded.
Hermes: How?
Trygaeus: How? In a swoon, because he couldn't survive the
sight of a cask full of wine smashed to bits.[3]

It was in irritation at this, it seems, that even though he had
retired from competition and writing, he wrote a play once again,
the *Wine Flask*, about himself and drunkenness, which employed
the following outline: Cratinus pretended that Comedy was his
wife but wanted to get a divorce from him, and she filed a lawsuit
against him for mistreatment. But Cratinus' friends happened by
and begged her not to do anything rash, and they asked the
reason for her hostility. She criticized the fact that he no longer
wrote comedies but wasted time with drunkenness.[4]

> I like the humor of the cask,
> the drunken blocked poet's plight,
> the comedy of a Comedy wife.
> Likewise, the drunk who spoke in
> his own defense, who wrote himself
> into his task.

Then he remembered Cratinus …
You couldn't have a drinking party without a chorus of "fig-
sandaled Doro," or "craftsmen of dexterous hymns." That's
how he flourished.
But today you see him a raving lunatic yet have no pity,
his ambers have fallen out, the string missing,
gaps in his scales. The old man wanders around,
like connas*, dying of thirst, his garland dried-up,
whose earlier victories deserve public payment of his tavern bills,

not babbling, but spectating in splendor in the audience,
beside Dionysus.[5] [*prizewinning pipe player, now a poor
drunk]

> I'm wont to say it's good to have a
> telling legacy, even one that speaks
> to twenty-five hundred years of debauchery.

[1] *Palatine Anthology* 13.29 (a line of an epigram derived from Cratinus,
according to Horace, *Epistles* 1.19.3 and other sources).
[2] Scholia on Aristophanes, *Knights* 526 ("flowing with great praise"):
Aristophanes seems to me to have taken the turn of phrase from what
Cratinus said in boasting about himself; for in *Wine Flask* he praised
himself something like this …
[3] Cratinus of Athens won a victory [best comedy] after the eighty-fifth
Olympiad [440-437] and died during the first Spartan invasion of Attica, as
Aristophanes says … Aristophanes, *Peace* 700-3.
[4] Scholia on Aristophanes, *Clouds*.
[5] Aristophanes, *Knights* 526-36.

* *Suda* kappa 2344:
Cratinus son of Callimedes, Athenian, writer of comedies. Brilliant in style, a
lover of drink with a weakness for pretty boys. He belonged to Old Comedy.
He wrote twenty-one plays, and won nine victories.
* Lucian, *Long-Lived Men* 25:
Cratinus the poet of comedy lived for ninety-four years, and at the end of his
life he was didaskalos [poet] for *Wine Flask* and won first prize, dying not
long after.

A Staggering Homeric
Befuddlement [156]

> I think some we meet may disapprove,
> that I'm wandering around drunk at a time like this.
> What torch is there, by the gods,
> so delightful as the sun?*

The Ridge Monte Bello would be my
Downfall; an unmixed oblivion blast off.
How they managed to rage all night puzzles
Me. I was shut down early with no
Utterance of any sort tripping past my
Purple lips. Silent purple stained words I
Hardly could think to speak, garbled
implosive thoughts, words lost in purple
shadows, and then you really don't care.

I think I may have been a drunk.

[*Athenaeus 15.700A; and in *One Possessed* Alexis writes …]

Greek Shade [157]

> I don't know exactly what it is, but nonetheless
> it's something like this, and I'm close to naming it.*

I may have said it: "this is like that,"
but I've yet to name anything.

And I know lots of things that have
no name. They tend to be red. I
just say "Those red things."

Worse, I don't even know exactly
what "I don't know exactly what it is"
means. But if I were close to naming it

I'd probably blurt out something like
"Mad taxonomic Greeks!"

And in this instance he's talking about
Eros. I'm no fool. I've got nothing to
say about that god.

This is a cold dark fate for an Attic Greek:
my heterogeneous world of unnamed things.

*Athenaeus 13.562A. From Alexis' comedy, *Phaedrus*, as quoted by one of
the diner guests in Athenaeus' multi-volume dialogue, *Deipnosophistai*
[*Intellectuals at Dinner*]. See 154, above.

                    The Shock of
                    Recognition [158]

There's a persistent shock of recognition with these
Greeks. More so for him, being ever vigilant for the
outré remark. Is that ironic? That here among forlorn
fragments and suggestive testimonia, our outsider—not
much more than a scholiast's marginal note—finds a
home?

But never in the chorus.

        Just as in a chorus.
    They don't all sing, but two or three, say, don't open their
    mouths,
    stand farthest away, and fill up the number,
    that's the way it is here: some people don't have a life,
    and some just take up space.
    [Menander, *Heiress* (fr. 130)]

A Comic Poet's Papyri* [159]

t would be quite somethi   he best
ords in the tex turned ou   e those
alling withi racketed ellipses […].**
've got crum   ng papyrus scraps
apyrus man   ipts from Egypt
tten in Gr k]; we   ke do, offering up
arly gu   es to fill e gaps and
ssing lin   f verse [ ]. But we can't
et too cre   e. We need to keep it
ight. But   how can we not?
Like, how   f verse do we
think are   missing here? Can't
we at le   easoned guess? Or,
given th   zard context, what
word cou   is be that be ith 'φ'?
We kno   some of his ot   tant
ems that our poet would of   such
with a learned flouris   not
nd we have stylistic   even
onal; we have our   tical
ur own familiar   this genre,
our poet. What gnaws at us is the
t somewhere (in a tomb, in
the Egyptian desert) there's
papyrus text (possibl ven wrapped
mmy—a 'textual' car nnage)
ased apart, will reveal a asure trove
ords and lines of verse n freed to
ir entombment, their liter mbalmment.
s always been this implicit nection
mortality in the accidental cho

ich scraps of papyrus text to recycl
    fate has deemed worthy of surviva
    he Oxyrhynchus Papyri]. Papyri,
   exts dead to us, brought back to life
 ; though the immortal may become lost,
  y are never dead].**

* See Appendix.

** Common scholarly practice: the crux [†] is used to designate corrupt text, a bracketed ellipsis […] to indicate gaps, and a bracketed space [ ] to mark the approximate text filled in by conjecture. Square brackets are also used to mark editorial insertions in the fragments.

8
....

THE ORDER IN WHICH
THEY CAME - 4

Adorno Parataxis [160]

preponderance of the object
the non-conceptual in the concept
consciousness of non-identity
totalizing ambitions of modern subjectivity
weak and fallible thinker
metaphysical pathos
illusion of concretization
delusion of constitutive subjectivity
belly turned mind
infantile fantasies of a primal return
separate the wild from the peaceful
rationalized rage against the non-identical
existential thinking crawls into the cave of a long-past mimesis
conceptual fetishism
chained to the cliff of their past
reification is forgetting
to the very borders of the dialectical insight into the non-
    identity in identity
free from the subjective spell
uncritical affirmation of givenness or sheer positivity
betrays utopia to imprisonment in selfhood
a life that is perverted in thingly form
autarky of the concept
where irreducible reality breaks in upon it
explode in miniature the mass of merely existing reality

the Whole is the Untrue
mimetic moment
the impossibility of reducing the real to its concept
caught up in a determining objectivity
an utterly impossible thing, a standpoint removed, even
    though by a hair's breadth from the scope of existence
disenchantment of the concept is the antidote of philosophy
the non-identical is the hinge of negative dialectics

            you must say words,
            as long as there are any* [161]

I'm being careful with my words, parsimonious, frugal,
using as few as possible. But as long as they last I'll
continue to speak, drawing upon my emergency cache
as they dwindle down to naught. Those last few words,
my last words, whichever words they be.

In the end, the last human words uttered, the last spoken
words, were … unknown, since only a speaker was left
to hear them. Thus the Era of Unknowns also came to
an end [*terminus ad quem*].
[*Samuel Beckett. *The Unnamable.*]

            Alphaville* [162]

peo pleh avebe comesl avestop robabili tysavetho sewhoweepw
ear euni quewr etched lyuniqu edoyoukn owwhattur
nsdarkness int olig htpoe tryalm ostever ydayword sdisappear
bec ause theya reforb iddenso sometime storeplac ethemtheyp
uti nnew words thatre present newideas overthepa sttwoorthr
eem onth ssome wordsi wasvery fondofdi sappeared robinredbr
eas twee pautu mnligh ttender nesstooe verything ishaphazar
dal lwor dsare sponta neousir efusetob ecomewhat youreferto

asn orma lthos ewhoha venotbe enborndo notcryand
havenoregr ets capi taled eladou leurtha tsallthe reistosay
unlessword sch ange their meanin gsandme aningsch angetheir
words
[*Jean-Luc Godard. *Alphaville*. 1965.]

Pragmatics [163]

We seem to have reached a dead end
Do you have anything to add
I've said all I'm going to say
I've heard that one before
Just one last thing
Nice speech
So you've said
Blah, blah, blah
What's that supposed to mean
I can't believe you just said that
I don't want to hear another word
Have you been listening to your self
What can I say to make you understand
I'll listen when you have something to say
I have no idea what you're trying to tell me
I'm only going to say this once
Can't you just tell me
I've already told you
You never listen
Don't lie to me
Just say it

There's not much point in going on
Feel better now

Tiananmen Square [164]

June 4th marks the thirtieth anniversary of

[CONTENT REMOVED BY AUTHOR]

\\\

Spanning Julys [165]

I've been nosing around this forgotten month sorting
mid-summer days and nights into rival camps:
   early dawn—how evenings linger,
   brightest green confusions—blues somber certitude,
   pool side chlorine—nights of billowing curtains,
   singing cicadas—glowing fireflies, white sparklers,
   sun in my face endless highway—no one's up on my street,
   grilled cheese sandwich with pickles and three Mickey's Big
   Mouths—a joint and two Pink's chili dogs,
   or ... drunk by noon—circling sobriety by midnight,
   coo-OO-oo-oo—ceaseless ringing in my ears,
   solitude—never ending, riotously populated dreams,
   scratchy three day lost weekend stubble—the snugged up
   mountains of Venus,
   slinking past embarrassment—please, not again,
   left home, walking—no one notices my return,
my inclination is not to speak—the urge overwhelms me.

With No Direction Home [166]

He once tried to join a Mathematical Club with no phone
number and a bogus address. That was the same year he got
lost in the mountains outside Telluride while attending the
Neuromorphic Engineering Workshop. Even got lost looking
for the bright kid's Puzzle Camp.

I was on the last fishing boat off the island just before Krakatoa
blew its top. Up the street having breakfast at Victor's when
that Boeing 767 struck the north tower at the World Trade
Center. Called in sick the day Viral-D escaped the safe room
at Pfizer. Being always a bit late or a bit early, absent or in the
wrong seat, I've been fate's elusive prey, just don't stand next to
me. [Doug Stewart. *1965.*]

The night he found himself trapped on a dead end street in Venice driving the car he'd stolen from the parking lot next to Whole Foods after watching *Bob le Flambeur* at the Aero in Santa Monica. Later, when they booked him, a smartass cop said, "You sure it wasn't *Touch of Evil*?"

The last time we spoke he said he'd put together a group of survivalists up by Bishop in the Eastern Sierras. They were in town—down in San Pedro, actually—buying up cargo containers they could repurpose as sturdy shelters for the coming end times. "You mean Boomervilles? With all those angry old people who listen only to the Dead?" "Well-*armed* angry old people," he said.

The Vengeful Croupier [167]

It's summer; I'm in Deauville for
the races. But baffled by the odds
I quickly burn through most of my
stake.

That evening, chasing my luck,
I walk over to the Casino from
the Hippodrome, where, unlike Bob,
I quickly lose the rest.

Nothing left, drunk at dawn, I'm
prostrate on the green baize table.
Stiffed by a vengeful croupier: life,
the fates, the endless game of who's
dealt in and who's dealt out.

Opening Day [168]

Smooth betting in lanes
of broken stone, a few
dollars in the rubble.

It's been thirty years [July 12, 1989 – July 17, 2019]
since my first opening day at Del Mar. This is how it
went today [winner and what I won*]:
    Julius [$3.60]
    United [$5.60]
    Avanti Bello [0.00]
    Facts Matter [$7.80]
    Storming Lady [$0.00]
    Freedom Ride [$8.60]
    Smiling Shirlee [$0.00]
    Jasikan [$5.80]
    King Jack [$4.80]
    Give Me the Lute [$0.00]
    [*81% ROI]

Betting no longshots,
a formful day of crushing chalk,
just timid smart play.

Self-Destructive Habits [169]

Filmic Los Angeles … passive city … a hundred destructions
… earthquakes … fires … volcanoes … tornados … lava flows
… tsunami … plagues … zombies … insects … aliens …
death rays … AI … sharks … replicants … pod people … and
things will crumble away through inattention.

Nemesis [170]

out from under the resinous pines
for the Perseids, out in the darkness
a blank-faced universe she couldn't
care less about:
       he wonders if endings aren't her specialty
       he knows she's fearless
       he tries to turn her attention elsewhere

Last Act [171]

Turned out after midnight
       with his jazz club women,
tripping cracked concrete
       sidewalks and dark stairwell
giggles with clasping hands
       at his back stopped rigid like
stage-struck. Last act, the
       perennial sick for sleep early
morning denouement in harsh
       sun bleaching light.

Sushi [172]

       They were co-workers stuck in
tedious occupational days of
       regimented hours but freed at
noon she'd wait in line for food
       truck sushi. Surprised that day,
caught by the rain, then back in
       his car she's rushed and flush-faced;
tidied up, she's hungry all afternoon.

Adrift [173]

Adrift when he surfaced from the sea of women,
he used his sunstone [*sólarsteinn*] to find the way.

Keywords:
mythical creatures
castaway
fleeing
darkness
caves
subterranean currents
holding one's breath
talisman
navigation

I [174]

Lost in her dog-eared lies.
Enveloped in gray-misted memories.
She's wondering: Do you remember me?

Can't [175]

A shaky hermeneutic with no point of view.
Disparate people spouting truisms left and right.
Dissimilar enough to mark several new species.

Hear You [176]

Diverging streams forcibly channeled into a torrent.
Overlapping waves in conforming quanta.
Deafening phonons in their cacophonous multitudes.

Maladies Philosophiques* [177]

Rooting around trash heaps
nosing out concepts frequently
laced with virulent green mold.

It took a certain amount
of desperation
to overcome the gagging.

And then the lingering illness:
   night sweats,
   nausea,
   confusional states.

The austere spa regimen:
   purgatives,
   steamed vegetables,
   long walks,
   talking cures
   [*consultation philosophique*].

Come bright autumn
semi-invalided out:
   no cure,
   no regrets.

Leaving us
to fend off
the contagion.
[*see: *Le manuel international des maladies philosophiques.* PUF, 1965.]

The Joke's Paper Thin [178]

I'm writing everything down on papyrus. I've
pulled down all my cloud texts and hired a dozen
scribes to commit everything to paper, ASAP.
My bet, I'm betting on a collapse akin to that of
the classical world, but with no Byzantine backups.

Server farms kaput, ice cold electrical grids,
technology's mechanisms now mere lumps of plastics
and rare earth metals. Like a sunny afternoon, this
era ends in darkness.

Someone here in the compound told me they've
heard of this prescient savant who's been babbling
on about history's last keystrokes. That it's a snap,
zap, and just like that not even enough time for
a farewell tweet.

So we're keeping busy, I've got them scribbling away
all day, and who knows, maybe someday they'll refer
to this as *my* house of papyri. I know those papyrological
archaeologists are going to be very excited when they
discover it.

Damnatio Memoriae [179]

by now
there's a lot of you

your simulacra
your digital abodes and representations
those innumerable messy traces [your muddy
footprints] you've left behind on the Web

if we could track all of you down
erase, delete this other you whose existence
is much less concrete than you imagine …
oh! there you go, or the larger part of you just did
and of you that's left [there is something?]
we're going to forget about that too

the condemnation of memory: for some of us would
hardly be punishment

El Rey del Tornado
[*Der Tornadokönig*] [180]

Troubled youth raised in a back-alley cyclone [*turbinis vasti*]
town, the future twisters [*puting beliung*] king of tornado
[*kimbunga*] alley. The Tornado King [*Le Roi Tornade*].]
[Spanish, German, Latin, Malay, Swahili, French]

The Tornado King [181]

Troubled youth raised in a back-alley
cyclone town, the future twisters king of
tornado alley.
The Tornado King.

APPENDIX

....

It would be quite something if the best
words in the text turned out to be those
falling within bracketed ellipses […].
We've got crumbling papyrus scraps
[papyrus manuscripts from Egypt
written in Greek]; we make do, offering up
scholarly guesses to fill the gaps and
missing lines of verse [ ]. But we can't
get too creative. We need to keep it
tight. But really, how can we not?
Like, how many lines of verse do we
think are actually missing here? Can't
we at least make a reasoned guess? Or,
given this haphazard context, what
word could this be that begins with 'φ'?
We know from some of his other extant
poems that our poet would often end such
a line with a learned flourish, so why not
here? And we have stylistics, maybe even
computational; we have our own critical
acumen, our own familiarity with this genre,
his era, our poet. What gnaws at us is the
knowledge that somewhere [in a tomb, in
a museum, in the Egyptian desert] there's
a scrap of papyrus text [possibly even wrapped
around a mummy—a 'textual' cartonnage]
that, teased apart, will reveal a treasure trove
of new words and lines of verse now freed to
flee their entombment, their literary embalmment.
There's always been this implicit connection
with immortality in the accidental choice

of which scraps of papyrus text to recycle
or that fate has deemed worthy of survival
[e.g., The Oxyrhynchus Papyri]. Papyri,
lost texts dead to us, brought back to life
[no; though the immortal may become lost,
they are never dead].

www.ingramcontent.com/pod-product-compliance
Lightning Source LLC
Chambersburg PA
CBHW060631130626
46555CB00002B/757

9781733493901